The Big Carrot

Written by Alison Hawes

Illustrated by Stuart Trotter

OXFORD
UNIVERSITY PRESS

Can Tom get the big carrot?

Tug!

Tom and Ifra
tug the big carrot.

Tom, Ifra and Nick tug.

Tom, Ifra, Nick and Lin tug.

Tom, Ifra, Nick, Lin
and Sam tug.

Tom, Ifra,
Nick, Lin,
Sam and Kit tug.

Tug!!!

Tug!

Up pops the big carrot!

Once upon a time...

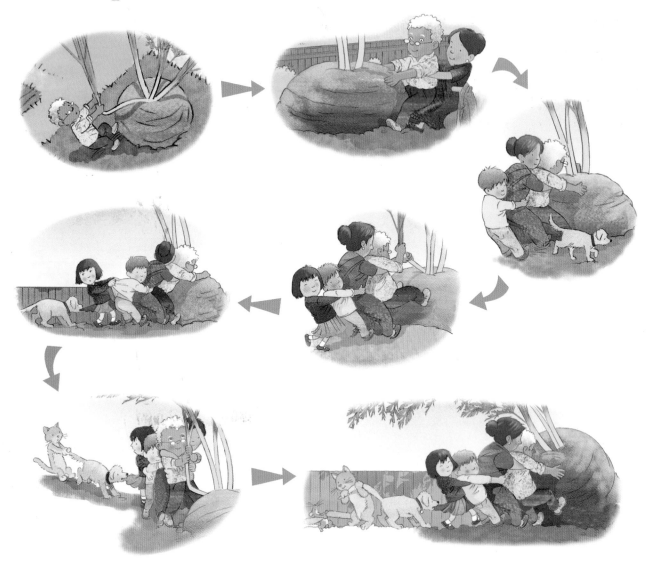

The end.